A Political Romance

Laurence Sterne

Contents

A POLITICAL ROMANCE

BY

Laurence Sterne

A Political Romance,
Addressed To _____ _____, Esq;
of York.
To which is subjoined a KEY.

Ridiculum acri Fortius et melius magnas plerumque secat Res

YORK: Printed in the Year MDCCLIX.
[Price ONE SHILLING.]

A POLITICAL ROMANCE, ETC.

SIR,

In my last, for want of something better to write about, I told you what a World of Fending and Proving we have had of late, in this little Village of ours, about an old-cast-Pair-of-black-Plush-Breeches, which John, our Parish-Clerk, about ten Years ago, it seems, had made a Promise of to one Trim, who is our Sexton and Dog-Whipper.--To this you write me Word, that you have had more than either one or two Occasions to know a good deal of the shifty Behaviour of this said Master Trim,-- and that you are astonished, nor can you for your Soul conceive, how so worthless a Fellow, and so worthless a Thing into the Bargain, could become the Occasion of such a Racket as I have represented.

Now, though you do not say expressly, you could wish to hear any more about it, yet I see plain enough that I have raised your Curiosity; and therefore, from the same Motive, that I slightly mentioned it at all in my last Letter, I will, in this, give you a full and very circumstantial Account of the whole Affair.

But, before I begin, I must first set you right in one very material Point, in which I have misled you, as to the true Cause of all this Uproar amongst us;--which does not take its Rise, as I then told you, from the Affair of the Breeches;--but, on the contrary, the whole Affair of the Breeches has taken its Rise from it:--To understand which, you must know, that the first Beginning of the Squabble was not between John the Parish-Clerk and Trim the Sexton, but betwixt the Parson of the Parish and the said Master Trim, about an old Watch-Coat, which had many Years hung up in the Church, which Trim had set his Heart upon; and nothing would serve Trim but he must take it home, in order to have it converted into a warm Under-Petticoat for his Wife, and a Jerkin for himself, against Winter; which, in a plaintive Tone, he most humbly begg'd his Reverence would consent to.

I need not tell you, Sir, who have so often felt it, that a Principle of strong Compassion transports a generous Mind sometimes beyond what is strictly right,--the Parson was within an Ace of being an honourable Example of this very Crime;--for no sooner did the distinct Words-- Petticoat--poor Wife--warm--Winter strike upon his Ear, but his Heart warmed,--and, before Trim had well got to the End of his Petition, (being a Gentleman of a frank and open Temper) he told him he was welcome to it, with all his Heart and Soul. But, Trim, says he, as you see I am but just got down to my Living, and am an utter Stranger to all Parish-Matters, know nothing about this old Watch-Coat you beg of me, having never seen it in my Life, and therefore cannot be a Judge whether 'tis fit for such a Purpose; or, if it is, in Truth, know not whether 'tis mine to bestow upon you or not;--you must have a Week or ten Days Patience, till I can make some Inquiries about it;--and, if I find it is in my Power, I tell you again, Man, your Wife is heartily welcome to an Under-Petticoat out of it, and you to a Jerkin, was the Thing as good again as you represent it.

It is necessary to inform you, Sir, in this Place, That the Parson was earnestly bent to serve Trim in this Affair, not only from the Motive of Generality, which I have justly ascribed to him, but likewise from another Motive; and that was by way of making some Sort of Recompence for a Multitude of small Services which Trim had occasionally done, and indeed was continually doing, (as he was much about the House) when his own Man was out of the Way. For all these Reasons together, I say, the Parson of the Parish intended to serve Trim in this Matter to the utmost of his Power: All that was wanting was previously to inquire, if any one had a Claim to it;--or whether, as it had, Time immemorial, hung up in the Church, the taking it down might not raise a Clamour in the Parish. These Inquiries were the very Thing that Trim dreaded in his Heart--He knew very well that if the Parson should but say one Word to the Church- Wardens about it, there would be an End of the whole Affair. For this, and some other Reasons not necessary to be told you, at present, Trim was for allowing no Time in this Matter;--but, on the contrary, doubled his Diligence and Importunity at the Vicarage-House;--plagued the whole Family to Death;--pressed his Suit Morning, Noon, and Night; and, to shorten my Story, teazed the poor Gentleman, who was but in an ill State of Health, almost out of his Life about it.

You will not wonder, when I tell you, that all this Hurry and Precipitation, on the Side of Master Trim, produced its natural Effect on the Side of the Parson, and that was, a Suspicion that all was not right at the Bottom.

He was one Evening sitting alone in his Study, weighing and turning this Doubt every Way in his Mind; and, after an Hour and a half's serious Deliberation upon the Affair, and running over Trim's Behaviour throughout,--he was just saying to himself, It must be so;--when a sudden Rap at the Door put an End to his Soliloquy,--and, in a few Minutes, to his Doubts too; for a Labourer in the Town, who deem'd himself past his fifty-second Year, had been returned by the Constable in the Militia-List,--and he had come, with a Groat in his Hand, to search the Parish Register for his Age.--The Parson bid the poor Fellow put the Groat into his Pocket, and go into the Kitchen:--Then shutting the Study Door, and taking down the Parish Register,--Who knows, says he, but I may find something here about this self-same Watch-Coat?--He had scarce unclasped the Book, in saying this, when he popp'd upon the very Thing he wanted, fairly wrote on the first Page, pasted to the Inside of one of the Covers, whereon was a Memorandum about the very Thing in Question, in these express Words:

MEMORANDUM.

The great Watch-Coat was purchased and given above two hundred years ago, by the Lord of the Manor, to this Parish-Church, to the sole use and Behoof of the poor sextons thereof, and their Sucessors, for ever, to be Worn by them respectively in wintery cold Nights, in ringing Complines, Passing-Bells, &c. which the said Lord of the manor had done, in Piety, to keep the poor Wretches warm, and for the Good of his own Soul, for Which they were directed to pray, &c. &c. &c. &c. Just

Heaven! said the Parson to himself, looking upwards, What an Escape have I had! Give this for an Under-Petticoat to Trim's Wife! I would not have consented to such a Desecration to be Primate of all England; nay, I would not have disturb'd a single Button of it for half my Tythes!

Scarce were the Words out of his Mouth, when in pops Trim with the whole Subject of the Exclamation under both his Arms.--I say, under both his Arms;--for he had actually got it ripp'd and cut out ready, his own Jerkin under one Arm, and the Petticoat under the other, in order to be carried to the Taylor to be made up,-- and had just stepp'd in, in high Spirits, to shew the Parson how cleverly it had held out.

There are many good Similies now subsisting in the World, but which I have neither Time to recollect or look for, which would give you a strong Conception of the Astonishment and honest Indignation which this unexpected Stroke of Trim's Impudence impress'd upon the Parson's Looks.--Let it suffice to say, That it exceeded all fair Description,-- as well as all Power of proper Resentment,--except this, that Trim was ordered, in a stern Voice, to lay the Bundles down upon the Table,--to go about his Business, and wait upon him, at his Peril, the next Morning at Eleven precisely,:--Against this Hour, like a wise Man, the Parson had sent to desire John the Parish-Clerk, who bore an exceeding good Character as a Man of Truth, and who having, moreover, a pretty Freehold of about eighteen Pounds a Year in the Township, was a leading Man in it; and, upon the whole, was such a one of whom it might be said,--That he rather did Honour to his Office,--than that his Office did Honour to him.--Him he sends for, with the Church-Wardens, and one of the Sides- Men, a grave, knowing, old Man, to be present:--For as Trim had withheld the whole Truth from the Parson, touching the Watch-Coat, he thought it probable he would as certainly do the same Thing to others; though this, I said, was wise, the Trouble of the Precaution might have been spared, --because the Parson's Character was unblemish'd,--and he had ever been held by the World in the Estimation of a Man of Honour and Integrity.-- Trim's Character, on the contrary, was as well known, if not in the World, yet, at least, in all the Parish, to be that of a little, dirty, pimping, pettifogging, ambidextrous Fellow,--who neither cared what he did or said of any, provided he could get a Penny by it.--This might, I say, have made any Precaution needless;--but you must know, as the Parson had in a Manner but just got down to his Living, he dreaded the Consequences of the least ill Impression on his first Entrance amongst his Parishioners, which would have disabled him from doing them the Good he Wished;--so that, out of Regard to his Flock, more than the necessary Care due to himself,--he was resolv'd not to lie at the Mercy of what Resentment might vent, or Malice lend an Ear to.--Accordingly the whole Matter was rehearsed from first to last by the Parson, in the Manner I've told you, in the Hearing of John the Parish-Clerk, and in the Presence of Trim.

Trim had little to say for himself, except "That the Parson had absolutely promised to befriend him and his Wife in the Affair, to the utmost of his Power: That the Watch-Coat was certainly in his Power, and that he might give it him if he pleased."

To this, the Parson's Reply was short, but strong, "That nothing was in his Power to do, but what he could do honestly:--That in giving the Coat to him and his Wife, he should do a manifest Wrong to the next Sexton; the great Watch-Coat being the most comfortable Part of the Place:--That he should, moreover, injure the Right of his own Successor, who would be just so much a worse Patron, as the Worth of the Coat amounted to;--and, in a Word, he declared, that his whole intent in promising that Coat, was Charity to Trim; but Wrong to no Man; that was a Reserve, he said, made in all Cases of this Kind:--and he declared solemnly, in Verbo Sacerdotis, That this was his Meaning, and was so understood by Trim himself."

With the Weight of this Truth, and the great good Sense and strong Reason which accompanied all the Parson said upon the Subject,--poor Trim was driven to his last Shift,--and begg'd he might be suffered to plead his Right and Title to the Watch-Coat, if not by Promise, at least by Services.--It was well known how much he was entitled to it upon these Scores: That he had black'd the Parson's Shoes without Count, and greased his Boots above fifty Times:--That he had run for Eggs into the Town upon all Occasions;--whetted the Knives at all Hours;--catched his Horse and rubbed him down:--That for his Wife she had been ready upon all Occasions to charr for them;--and neither he nor she, to the best of his Remembrance, ever took a Farthing, or any thing beyond a Mug of Ale.--To this Account of his Services he begg'd Leave to add those of his Wishes, which, he said, had been equally great.-- He affirmed, and was ready, he said, to make it appear, by Numbers of Witnesses, "He had drank his Reverence's Health a thousand Times, (by the bye, he did not add out of the Parson's own Ale): That he not only drank his Health, but wish'd it; and never came to the House, but ask'd his Man kindly how he did; that in particular, about half a Year ago, when his Reverence cut his Finger in paring an Apple, he went half a Mile to ask a cunning Woman, what was good to stanch Blood, and actually returned with a Cobweb in his Breeches Pocket:--Nay, says Trim, it was not a Fortnight ago, when your Reverence took that violent Purge, that I went to the far End of the whole Town to borrow you a Close-stool,--and came back, as my Neighbours, who flouted me, will all bear witness, with the Pan upon my Head, and never thought it too much."

Trim concluded his pathetick Remonstrance with saying, "He hoped his Reverence's Heart would not suffer him to requite so many faithful Services by so unkind a Return:--That if it was so, as he was the first, so he hoped he should be the last, Example of a Man of his Condition so treated."--This Plan of Trim's Defence, which Trim had put himself upon,--could admit of no other Reply but a general Smile.

Upon the whole, let me inform you, That all that could be said, pro and con, on both Sides, being fairly heard, it was plain, That Trim, in every Part of this Affair, had behaved very ill;--and one Thing, which was never expected to be known of him, happening in the Course of this Debate to come out against him; namely, That he had gone and told the Parson, before he had ever set Foot in his Parish, That John his Parish- Clerk,--his Church-Wardens, and some of the Heads of the Parish, were a Parcel of Scoundrels.--Upon the Upshot, Trim was kick'd out of Doors; and told, at his Peril, never to come there again.

At first Trim huff'd and bounced most terribly;--swore he would get a Warrant;--then nothing would serve him but he would call a Bye-Law, and tell the whole Parish how the Parson had misused him;--but cooling of that, as fearing the Parson might possibly bind him over to his good Behaviour, and, for aught he knew, might send him to the House of Correction,--he let the Parson alone; and, to revenge himself, falls foul upon his Clerk, who had no more to do in the Quarrel than you or I;--rips up the Promise of the old-cast-Pair-of-black-Plush-Breeches, and raises an Uproar in the Town about it, notwithstanding it had slept ten Years.--But all this, you must know, is look'd upon in no other Light, but as an artful Stroke of Generalship in Trim, to raise a Dust, and cover himself under the disgraceful Chastisement he has undergone.

If your Curiosity is not yet satisfied,--I will now proceed to relate the Battle of the Breeches, in the same exact Manner I have done that of the Watch-Coat.

Be it known then, that, about ten Years ago, when John was appointed Parish-Clerk of this Church, this said Master Trim took no small Pains to get into John's good Graces in order, as it afterwards appeared, to coax a Promise out of him of a Pair of Breeches, which John had then by him, of black Plush, not much the worse for wearing;--Trim only begging for God's Sake to have them bestowed upon him when John should think fit to cast them.

Trim was one of those kind of Men who loved a Bit of Finery in his Heart, and would rather have a tatter'd Rag of a Better Body's, than the best plain whole Thing his Wife could spin him.

John, who was naturally unsuspicious, made no more Difficulty of promising the Breeches, than the Parson had done in promising the Great Coat; and, indeed, with something less Reserve,--because the Breeches were John's own, and he could give them, without Wrong, to whom he thought fit.

It happened, I was going to say unluckily, but, I should rather say, most luckily, for Trim, for he was the only Gainer by it;--that a Quarrel, about some six or eight Weeks after this, broke out between the late Parson of the Parish and John the Clerk. Somebody (and it was thought to be Nobody but Trim) had put it into the Parson's Head, "That John's Desk in the Church was, at the least, four Inches higher than it should be:--That the Thing gave Offence, and was indecorous, inasmuch as it approach'd too near upon a Level with the Parson's Desk itself." This Hardship the Parson complained of loudly,--and told John one Day after Prayers, "He could bear it no longer:--And would have it alter'd and brought down as it should be." John made no other Reply, but, "That the Desk was not of his raising:--That 'twas not one Hair Breadth higher than he found it;--and that as he found it, so would he leave it:--In short, he would neither make an Encroachment, nor would he suffer one."

The late Parson might have his Virtues, but the leading Part of his Character was not Humility; so that John's Stiffness in this Point was not likely to reconcile Matters.--This was Trim's Harvest.

After a friendly Hint to John to stand his Ground,--away hies Trim to make his Market at the Vicarage: What pass'd there, I will not say, intending not to be uncharitable; so shall content myself with only guessing at it, from the sudden Change that appeared in Trim's Dress for the better;--for he had left his old ragged Coat, Hat and Wig, in the Stable, and was come forth strutting across the Church-yard, y'clad in a good creditable cast Coat, large Hat and Wig, which the Parson had just given him.--Ho! Ho! Hollo! John! cries Trim, in an insolent Bravo, as loud as ever he could bawl--See here, my Lad! how fine I am.--The more Shame for you, answered John, seriously.--Do you think, Trim, says he, such Finery, gain'd by such Services, becomes you, or can wear well?-- Fye upon it, Trim;--I could not have expected this from you, considering what Friendship you pretended, and how kind I have ever been to you:-- How many Shillings and Sixpences I have generously lent you in your Distresses?--Nay, it was but t'other Day that I promised you these black Plush Breeches I have on.--Rot your Breeches, quoth Trim; for Trim's Brain was half turn'd with his new Finery:--Rot your Breeches, says he, --I would not take them up, were they laid at my Door;--give 'em, and be d----d to you, to whom you like; I would have you to know I can have a better Pair at the Parson's any Day in the Week:--John told him plainly, as his Word had once pass'd him, he had a Spirit above taking Advantage of his Insolence, in giving them away to another:--But, to tell him his Mind freely, he thought he had got so many Favours of that Kind, and was so likely to get many more for the same Services, of the Parson, that he had better give up the Breeches, with good Nature, to some one who would be more thankful for them.

Here John mentioned Mark Slender, (who, it seems, the Day before, had ask'd John for 'em) not knowing they were under Promise to Trim.--"Come, Trim, says he, let poor Mark have 'em,--You know he has not a Pair to his. A----: Besides, you see he is just of my Size, and they will fit him to a T; whereas, if I give 'em to you,--look ye, they are not worth much; and, besides, you could not get your Backside into them, if you had them, without tearing them all to Pieces."

Every Tittle of this was most undoubtedly true; for Trim, you must know, by foul Feeding, and playing the good Fellow at the Parson's, was grown somewhat gross about the lower Parts, if not higher: So that, as all John said upon the Occasion was fact, Trim, with much ado, and after a hundred Hum's and Hah's, at last, out of mere Compassion to Mark, signs, seals, and delivers up all Right, Interest, and Pretentions whatsoever, in and to the said breeches; thereby binding his Heirs, Executors, Administrators, and Assignes, never more to call the said Claim in Question.

All this Renunciation was set forth in an ample Manner, to be in pure Pity to Mark's Nakedness;--but the Secret was, Trim had an Eye to, and firmly expected in his own Mind, the great Green Pulpit-Cloth and old Velvet Cushion, which were that very Year to be taken down;--which, by the Bye, could he have wheedled John a second Time out of 'em, as he hoped, he had made up the Loss of his Breeches Seven-fold.

Now, you must know, this Pulpit-Cloth and Cushion were not in John's Gift, but in the Church-Wardens, &c.--However, as I said above, that John was a leading Man in the Parish, Trim knew he could help him to them if he would:--But John had got a Surfeit of him;--so, when the Pulpit-Cloth, &c. were taken down, they were immediately given (John having a great Say in it) to William Doe, who understood very well what Use to make of them.

As for the old Breeches, poor Mark Slender lived to wear them but a short Time, and they got into the Possession of Lorry Slim, an unlucky Wight, by whom they are still worn;--in Truth, as you will guess, they are very thin by this Time:--But Lorry has a light Heart; and what recommends them to him, is this, that, as, thin as they are, he knows that Trim, let him say what he will to the contrary, still envies the Possessor of them,--and, with all his Pride, would be very glad to wear them after him.

Upon this Footing have these Affairs slept quietly for near ten Years,-- and would have slept for ever, but for the unlucky Kicking-Bout; which, as I said, has ripp'd this Squabble up afresh: So that it was no longer ago than last Week, that Trim met and insulted John in the public Town- Way, before a hundred People;--tax'd him with the Promise of the old- cast-Pair-of-black-Breeches, notwithstanding Trim's solemn Renunciation; twitted him with the Pulpit-Cloth and Velvet Cushion,--as good as told him, he was ignorant of the common Duties of his Clerkship; adding, very insolently, That he knew not so much as to give out a common Psalm in Tune.--

John contented himself with giving a plain Answer to every Article that Trim had laid to his Charge, and appealed to his Neighbours who remembered the whole Affair;--and as he knew there was never any Thing to be got in wrestling with a Chimney-Sweeper,--he was going to take Leave of Trim for ever.--But, hold,--

the Mob by this Time had got round them, and their High Mightinesses insisted upon having Trim tried upon the Spot.--Trim was accordingly tried; and, after a full Hearing, was convicted a second Time, and handled more roughly by one or more of them, than even at the Parson's.

Trim, says one, are you not ashamed of yourself, to make all this Rout and Disturbance in the Town, and set Neighbours together by the Ears, about an old-worn-out-Pair-of-cast-Breeches, not worth Half a Crown?--Is there a cast-Coat, or a Place in the whole Town, that will bring you in a Shilling, but what you have snapp'd up, like a greedy Hound as you are?

In the first Place, are you not Sexton and Dog-Whipper, worth Three Pounds a Year?--Then you begg'd the Church-Wardens to let your Wife have the Washing and Darning of the Surplice and Church-Linen, which brings you in Thirteen Shillings and Four Pence.--Then you have Six Shillings and Eight Pence for oiling and winding up the Clock, both paid you at Easter.--The Pinder's Place, which is worth Forty Shillings a Year,--you have got that too.--You are the Bailiff, which the late Parson got you, which brings you in Forty Shillings more.--Besides all this, you have Six Pounds a Year, paid you Quarterly for being Mole-Catcher to the Parish.--Aye, says the luckless Wight above-mentioned, (who was standing close to him with his Plush Breeches on) "You are not only Mole-Catcher, Trim, but you catch STRAY CONIES too in the Dark; and you pretend a Licence for it, which, I trove, will be look'd into at the next Quarter Sessions." I maintain it, I have a Licence, says Trim, blushing as red as Scarlet:--I have a Licence,--and as I farm a Warren in the next Parish, I will catch Conies every Hour of the Night.--You catch Conies! cries a toothless old Woman, who was just passing by.--

This set the Mob a laughing, and sent every Man home in perfect good Humour, except Trim, who waddled very slowly off with that Kind of inflexible Gravity only to be equalled by one Animal in the whole Creation,--and surpassed by none, I am,

SIR, Yours, &c. &c.

FINIS.

POSTSCRIPT.

I have broke open my Letter to inform you, that I miss'd the Opportunity of sending it by the Messenger, who I expected would have called upon me in his Return through this Village to York, so it has laid a Week or ten Days by me. --I am not sorry for the Disappointment, because something has since happened, in Continuation of this Affair, which I am thereby enabled to transmit to you, all under one Trouble.

When I finished the above Account, I thought (as did every Soul in the Parish) Trim had met with so thorough a Rebuff from John the Parish-Clerk and the Town's Folks, who all took against him, that Trim would be glad to be quiet, and let the Matter rest.

But, it seems, it is not half an Hour ago since Trim sallied forth again; and, having borrowed a Sow-Gelder's Horn, with hard Blowing he got the whole Town round him, and endeavoured to raise a Disturbance, and fight the whole Battle over again:--That he had been used in the last Fray worse than a Dog;--not by John the Parish-Clerk,--for I shou'd not, quoth Trim, have valued him a Rush single Hands:--But all the Town sided with him, and twelve Men in Buckram set upon me all at once, and kept me in Play at Sword's Point for three Hours together.--Besides, quoth Trim, there were two misbegotten Knaves in Kendal Green, who lay all the while in Ambush in John's own House, and they all sixteen came upon my Back, and let drive at me together.--A Plague, says Trim, of all Cowards!--Trim repeated this Story above a Dozen Times;--which made some of the Neighbours pity him, thinking the poor Fellow crack-brain'd, and that he actually believed what he said. After this Trim dropp'd the Affair of the Breeches, and begun a fresh Dispute about the Reading-Desk, which I told you had occasioned some small Dispute between the late Parson and John, some Years ago.

This Reading-Desk, as you will observe, was but an Episode wove into the main Story by the Bye;--for the main Affair was the Battle of the Breeches and Great Watch-Coat.--However, Trim being at last driven out of these two Citadels,--he has seized hold, in his Retreat, of this Reading-Desk, with a View, as it seems, to take Shelter behind it.

I cannot say but the Man has fought it out obstinately enough;--and, had his Cause been good, I should have really pitied him. For when he was driven out of the Great Watch-Coat,--you see, he did not run away;--no, --he retreated behind the Breeches;--and, when he could make nothing of it behind the Breeches,--he got behind the Reading-Desk.--To what other Hold Trim will next retreat, the Politicians of this Village are not agreed.--Some think his next Move will be towards the Rear of the Parson's Boot;--but, as it is thought he cannot make a long Stand there,--others are of Opinion, That Trim will once more in his Life get hold of the Parson's Horse, and charge upon him, or perhaps behind him. But as the Horse is not easy to be caught, the more general Opinion is, That, when he is driven out of the Reading-Desk, he will make his last Retreat in such a Manner as, if possible, to gain the Close-Stool, and defend himself behind it to the very last Drop. If Trim should make this Movement, by my Advice he should be left besides his Citadel, in full Possession of the Field of Battle;--where, 'tis certain, he will keep every Body a League off, and may pop by himself till he is weary: Besides, as Trim seems bent upon purging himself, and may have Abundance of foul Humours to work off, I think he cannot be better placed.

But this is all Matter of Speculation.--Let me carry you back to Matter of Fact, and tell you what Kind of a Stand Trim has actually made behind the said Desk.

"Neighbours and Townsmen all, I will be sworn before my Lord Mayor, That John and his nineteen Men in Buckram, have abused me worse than a Dog; for they told you that I play'd fast and go-loose with the late Parson and him, in that old Dispute of theirs about the Reading-Desk; and that I made Matters worse between them, and not better."

Of this Charge, Trim declared he was as innocent as the Child that was unborn: That he would be Book-sworn he had no Hand in it. He produced a strong Witness;--and, moreover, insinuated, that John himself, instead of being angry for what he had done in it, had actually thank'd him. Aye, Trim, says the Wight in the

Plush Breeches, but that was, Trim, the Day before John found thee out.--Besides, Trim, there is nothing in that:--For, the very Year that thou wast made Town's Pinder, thou knowest well, that I both thank'd thee myself; and, moreover, gave thee a good warm Supper for turning John Lund's Cows and Horses out of my Hard-Corn Close; which if thou had'st not done, (as thou told'st me) I should have lost my whole Crop: Whereas, John Lund and Thomas Patt, who are both here to testify, and will take their Oaths on't, That thou thyself wast the very Man who set the Gate open; and, after all,--it was not thee, Trim,--'twas the Blacksmith's poor Lad who turn'd them out: So that a Man may be thank'd and rewarded too for a good Turn which he never did, nor ever did intend.

Trim could not sustain this unexpected Stroke;--so Trim march'd off the Field, without Colours flying, or his Horn sounding, or any other Ensigns of Honour whatever.

Whether after this Trim intends to rally a second Time, or whether Trim may not take it into his Head to claim the Victory,--no one but Trim himself can inform you:--However, the general Opinion, upon the whole, is this, That, in three several pitch'd Battles, Trim has been so trimm'd, as never disastrous Hero was trimm'd before him.

THE KEY.

This Romance was, by some Mischance or other, dropp'd in the Minster-Yard, York, and pick'd up by a Member of a small Political Club in that City; where it was carried, and publickly read to the Members the last Club Night.

It was instantly agreed to, by a great Majority, That it was a Political Romance; but concerning what State or Potentate, could not so easily be settled amongst them.

The President of the Night, who is thought to be as clear and quick- lighted as any one of the whole Club in Things of this Nature, discovered plainly, That the Disturbances therein set forth, related to those on the Continent:--That Trim could be Nobody but the King of France, by whole shifting and intriguing Behaviour, all Europe was set together by the Ears:--That Trim's Wife was certainly the Empress, who are as kind together, says he, as any Man and Wife can be for their Lives.--The more Shame for 'em, says an Alderman, low to himself.-- Agreeable to this Key, continues the President,--The Parson, who I think is a most excellent Character,--is His Most Excellent Majesty King George;--John, the Parish-Clerk, is the King of Prussia; who, by the Manner of his first entering Saxony, shew'd the World most evidently,-- That he did know how to lead out the Psalm, and in Tune and Time too, notwithstanding Trim's vile Insult upon him in that Particular.--But who do you think, says a Surgeon and Man-Midwife, who sat next him, (whose Coat-Button the President, in the Earnestness of this Explanation, had got fast hold of, and had thereby partly drawn him over to his Opinion) Who do you think, Mr. President, says he, are meant by the Church- Wardens, Sides-Men, Mark Slender, Lorry Slim, &c.--Who do I think? says he, Why,--Why, Sir, as I take the Thing,-- the Church-Wardens and Sides- Men, are the Electors and the other Princes who form the Germanick Body.--And as for the other subordinate Characters of Mark Slim,--the unlucky Wight in the Plush Breeches,--the Parson's Man who was so often out of the Way, &c. &c.--these, to be sure, are the several Marshals and Generals, who fought, or should have fought, under them the last Campaign.--The Men in Buckram, continued the President, are the Grofs of the King of Prussia's Army, who are as stiff a Body of Men as are in the World:--And Trim's saying they were twelve, and then nineteen, is a Wipe for the Brussels Gazetteer, who, to my Knowledge, was never two Weeks in the same Story, about that or any thing else.

As for the rest of the Romance, continued the President, it sufficiently explains itself,--The Old-cast-Pair-of-Black-Plush-Breeches must be Saxony, which the Elector, you see, has left of wearing:--And as for the Great Watch-Coat, which, you know, covers all, it signifies all Europe; comprehending, at least, so many of its different States and Dominions, as we have any Concern with in the present War.

I protest, says a Gentleman who sat next but one to the President, and who, it seems, was the Parson of the Parish, a Member not only of the Political, but also of a Musical Club in the next Street;--I protest, says he, if this Explanation is right, which I think it is, That the whole makes a very fine Symbol.--You have always some Musical Instrument or other in your Head, I think, says the Alderman.--Musical instrument! replies the Parson, in Astonishment,--Mr. Alderman, I mean an Allegory; and I think the greedy Disposition of Trim and his Wife, in ripping the Great Watch-Coat to Pieces, in order to convert it into a Petticoat for the one, and a Jerkin for the other, is one of the most beautiful of the Kind I ever met with; and will shew all the World what have been the true Views and Intentions of the Houses of Bourbon and Austria in this abominable Coalition,--I might have called it Whoredom:--Nay, says the Alderman, 'tis downright Adulterydom, or nothing.

This Hypothesis of the President's explain'd every Thing in the Romance extreamly well; and, withall, was delivered with so much Readiness and Air of Certainty, as begot an Opinion in two Thirds of the Club, that Mr. President was actually the Author of the Romance himself: But a Gentleman who sat on the opposite Side of the Table, who had come piping-hot from reading the History of King William's and Queen Anne's Wars, and who was thought, at the Bottom, to envy the President the Honour both of the Romance and Explanation too, gave an entire new Turn to it all. He acquainted the Club, That Mr. President was altogether wrong in every Supposition he had made, except that one, where the Great Watch-Coat was said by him to represent Europe, or at least a great Part of it:--So far he acknowledged he was pretty right; but that he had not gone far enough backwards into our History to come at the Truth. He then acquainted them, that the dividing the Great Watch-Coat did, and could, allude to nothing else in the World but the Partition-Treaty; which, by the Bye, he told them, was the most unhappy and scandalous Transaction in all King William's Life: It was that false Step, and that only, says he, rising from his Chair, and striking his Hand upon the Table with great Violence; it was that false Step, says he, knitting his Brows and throwing his Pipe down upon the Ground, that has laid the Foundation of all the Disturbances and Sorrows we feel and lament at this very Hour; and as for Trim's giving up the Breeches, look ye, it is almost Word for Word copied from the French King and Dauphin's Renunciation of Spain and the West-Indies, which all the World knew (as was the very Case of the Breeches) were renounced by them on purpose to be reclaim'd when Time should serve.

This Explanation had too much Ingenuity in it to be altogether slighted; and, in Truth, the worst Fault it had, seem'd to be the prodigious Heat of it; which (as an Apothecary, who sat next the Fire, observ'd, in a very low Whisper to his next Neighbour) was so much incorporated into every Particle of it, that it was impossible, under such Fermentation, it should work its defined Effect.

This, however, no way intimidated a little valiant Gentleman, though he sat the very next Man, from giving an Opinion as diametrically opposite as East is from West.

This Gentleman, who was by much the best Geographer in the whole Club, and, moreover, second Cousin to an Engineer, was positive the Breeches meant Gibraltar; for, if you remember, Gentlemen, says he, tho' possibly you don't, the Ichnography and Plan of that Town and Fortress, it exactly resembles a Pair of Trunk-Hose, the two Promontories forming the two Slops, &c. &c.--Now we all know, continued he, that King George the First made a Promise of that important Pass to the King of Spain:--So that the whole Drift of the Romance, according to my Sense of Things, is merely to vindicate the King and the Parliament in that Transaction, which made so much Noise in the World.

A Wholesale Taylor, who from the Beginning had resolved not to speak at all in the Debate,--was at last drawn into it, by something very unexpected in the last Person's Argument.

He told the Company, frankly, he did not understand what Ichnography meant:--But as for the Shape of a Pair of Breeches, as he had had the Advantage of cutting out so many hundred Pairs in his Life-Time, he hoped he might be allowed to know as much of the Matter as another Man.

Now, to my Mind, says he, there is nothing in all the Terraqueous Globe (a Map of which, it seems, hung up in his Work-Shop) so like a Pair of Breeches un-made up, as the Island of Sicily:--Nor is there any thing, if you go to that, quoth an honest Shoe-maker, who had the Honour to be a Member of the Club, so much like a Jack-Boot, to my Fancy, as the Kingdom of Italy.--What the Duce has either Italy or Sicily to do in the Affair? cries the President, who, by this Time, began to tremble for his Hypothesis,--What have they to do?--Why, answered the Partition-Treaty Gentleman, with great Spirit and Joy sparkling in his Eyes,--They have just so much, Sir, to do in the Debate as to overthrow your Suppositions, and to estab-lish the Certainty of mine beyond the Possibility of a Doubt: For, says he, (with an Air of Sovereign Triumph over the President's Politicks)--By the Partition-Treaty, Sir, both Naples and Sicily were the very Kingdoms made to devolve upon the Dauphin;--and Trim's greasing the Parson's Boots, is a Devilish Satyrical Stroke;--for it exposes the Corruption, and Bribery made Use of at that Juncture, in bringing over the several States and Princes of Italy to use their Interests at Rome, to stop the Pope from giving the Investitures of those Kingdoms to any Body else.--The Pope has not the Investiture of Sicily, cries another Gentleman.--I care not, says he, for that.

Almost every one apprehended the Debate to be now ended, and that no one Member would venture any new Conjecture upon the Romance, after so many clear and decisive Interpretations had been given. But, hold,--Close to the Fire, and oppo-site to where the Apothecary sat, there sat also a Gentleman of the Law, who, from the Beginning to the End of the Hearing of this Case, seem'd no way satisfied in his Conscience with any one Proceeding in it. This Gentleman had not yet opened his Mouth, but had waited patiently till they had all gone thro' their several Evidences on the other Side;--reserving himself, like an expert Practitioner, for the last Word in the Debate. When the Partition-Treaty-Gentleman had finish'd what he had to say,--He got up,--and, advancing towards the Table, told them, That the Error they had all gone upon thus far, in making out the several Facts in the Romance,--was in looking too high; which, with great Candor, he said, was a very natural Thing, and very excusable withall, in such a Political Club as theirs: For Instance, continues he, you have been searching the Registers, and looking into the Deeds of Kings and Emperors,--as if Nobody had any Deeds to shew or compare the Romance to but themselves.--This, continued the Attorney, is just as much out of the Way of good Practice, as if I should carry a Thing slap-dash into the House of Lords, which was under forty Shillings, and might be decided in the next County-Court for six Shillings and Eight-pence.--He then took the Romance in his Left Hand, and pointing with the Fore-Finger of his Right towards the second Page, he humbly begg'd Leave to observe, (and, to do him Justice, he did it in somewhat of a forensic Air) That the Parson, John, and Sexton, shewed incontestably the Thing to be Tripartite; now, if you will take Notice, Gentlemen, says he, these several Persons, who are Parties to this Instrument, are merely Ecclesiastical; that the Reading-Desk, Pulpit- Cloth, and Velvet Cushion, are tripartite too; and are, by Intendment of Law, Goods and Chattles merely of an Ecclesiastick Nature, belonging and appertaining 'only unto them,' and to them only.--So that it appears very plain to me, That the Romance, neither directly nor indirectly, goes upon Temporal, but altogether upon Church-Matters.--And do not you think, says he, softening his Voice a little, and addressing himself to the Parson with a forced Smile,--Do not you think Doctor, says he, That the Dispute in the Romance, between the Parson of the Parish and John, about the Height of John's Desk, is a very fine Panegyrick upon the Humility of Church-Men?--I think, says the Parson, it is much of the same Fineness with that which your Profession is complimented with, in the pimping, dirty, pettyfogging Character of Trim,--which, in my Opinion, Sir, is just such another Panegyrick upon the Honestly of Attornies.

Nothing whets the Spirits like an Insult:--Therefore the Parson went on with a visible Superiority and an uncommon Acuteness.--As you are so happy, Sir, continues he, in making Applications,--pray turn over a Page or two to the black Law-Letters in the Romance.--What do you think of them, Sir?--Nay,--pray read the Grant of the Great Watch-Coat and Trim's Renunciation of the Breeches.--Why, there is downright Lease and Release for you,--'tis the very Thing, Man;--only with this small Difference,-- and in which consists the whole Strength of the Panegyric, That the Author of the Romance has convey'd and re-convey'd, in about ten Lines, --what you, with the glorious Prolixity of the Law, could not have crowded into as many Skins of Parchment.

The Apothecary, who had paid the Attorney, the same Afternoon, a Demand of Three Pounds Six Shillings and Eight-Pence, for much such another Jobb,--was so highly tickled with the Parson's Repartee in that particular Point,--that he rubb'd his Hands together most fervently,-- and laugh'd most triumphantly thereupon.

This could not escape the Attorney's Notice, any more than the Cause of it did escape his Penetration.

I think, Sir, says he, (dropping his Voice a Third) you might well have spared this immoderate Mirth, since you and your Profession have the least Reason to triumph here of any of us.--I beg, quoth he, that you would reflect a Moment upon the Cob-Web which Trim went so far for, and brought back with an Air of so much Importance, in his Breeches Pocket, to lay upon the Parson's cut Finger.-- This said Cob-Web, Sir, is a fine- spun Satyre, upon the flimsy Nature of one Half of the Shop-Medicines, with which you make a Property of the Sick, the Ignorant, and the Unsuspecting.--And as for the Moral of the Close-Stool-Pan, Sir, 'tis too plain, Does not nine Parts in ten of the whole Practice, and of all you vend under its Colours, pass into and concenter in that one nasty Utensil?--And let me tell you, Sir, says he, raising his Voice,--had not your unseasonable Mirth blinded you, you might have seen that Trim's carrying the Close-Stool-Pan upon his Head the whole Length of the Town, without blushing, is a pointed Raillery,--and one of the sharpest Sarcasms, Sir, that ever was thrown out upon you;--for it unveils the solemn Impudence of the whole Profession, who, I see, are ashamed of nothing which brings in Money.

There were two Apothecaries in the Club, besides the Surgeon mentioned before, with a Chemist and an Undertaker, who all felt themselves equally hurt and aggrieved by this discourteous Retort:--And they were all five rising up together from their Chairs, with full Intent of Heart, as it was thought, to return the Reproof Valiant thereupon.--But the President, fearing it would end in a general Engagement, he instantly call'd out, To Order;--and gave Notice, That if there was any Member in the Club, who had not yet spoke, and yet did desire to speak upon the main Subject of the Debate,--that he should immediately be heard.

This was a happy Invitation for a stammering Member, who, it seems, had but a weak Voice at the best; and having often attempted to speak in the Debate, but to no Purpose, had sat down in utter Despair of an Opportunity.

This Member, you must know, had got a sad Crush upon his Hip, in the late Election, which gave him intolerable Anguish;--so that, in short, he could think of nothing else:--For which Cause, and others, he was strongly of Opinion, That the whole Romance was a just Gird at the late York Election; and I think, says he, that the Promise of the Breeches broke, may well and truly signify Somebody's else Promise, which was broke, and occasion'd to much Disturbance amongst us.

Thus every Man turn'd the Story to what was swimming uppermost in his own Brain;--so that, before all was over, there were full as many Satyres spun out of it,--and as great a Variety of Personages, Opinions, Transactions, and Truths, found to lay hid under the dark Veil of its Allegory, as ever were discovered in the thrice-renowned History of the Acts of Gargantua and Pantagruel.

At the Close of all, and just before the Club was going to break up,-- Mr. President rose from his Chair, and begg'd Leave to make the two following Motions, which were instantly agreed to, without any Division.

First Gentlemen, says he, as Trim's Character in the Romance, of a shuffling intriguing Fellow,--whoever it was drawn for, is, in Truth, as like the French King as it can stare,--I move, That the Romance be forthwith printed:--For, continues he, if we can but once turn the Laugh against him, and make him asham'd of what he has done, it may be a great Means, with the Blessing of God upon our Fleets and Armies, to save the Liberties of Europe.

In the second Place, I move, That Mr. Attorney, our worthy Member, be desired to take Minutes, upon the Spot, of every Conjecture which has been made upon the Romance, by the several Members who have spoke; which, I think, says he, will answer two good Ends:

1st, It will establish the Political Knowledge of our Club for ever, and place it in a respectable Light to all the World.

In the next Place, it will furnish what will be wanted; that is, a Key to the Romance.--In troth you might have said a whole Bunch of Keys, quoth a White-smith, who was the only Member in the Club who had not said something in the

Debate: But let me tell you, Mr. President, says he, That the Right Key, if it could but be found, would be worth the whole Bunch put together.

To ------ ---------, Esq; of York.

Sir,

You write me Word that the Letter I wrote to you, and now stiled The Political Romance is printing; and that, as it was drop'd by Carelessness, to make some Amends, you will overlook the Printing of it yourself, and take Care to see that it comes right into the World.

I was just going to return you Thanks, and to beg, withal, you would take Care That the Child be not laid at my Door.--But having, this Moment, perused the Reply to the Dean of York's Answer,--it has made me alter my Mind in that respect; so that, instead of making you the Request I intended, I do here desire That the Child be filiated upon me, Laurence Sterne, Prebendary of York, &c. &c. And I do, accordingly, own it for my own true and lawful Offspring.

My Reason for this is plain;--for as, you see, the Writer of that Reply, has taken upon him to invade this incontested Right of another Man's in a Thing of this Kind, it is high Time for every Man to look to his own-- Since, upon the same Grounds, and with half the Degree of Anger, that he affirms the Production of that very Reverend Gentleman's, to be the Child of many Fathers, some one in his Spight (for I am not without my Friends of that Stamp) may run headlong into the other Extream, and swear, That mine had no Father at all:--And therefore, to make use of Bays's Plea in the Rehearsal, for Prince Pretty-Man; I merely do it, as he says, "for fear it should be said to be no Body's Child at all."

I have only to add two Things:--First, That, at your Peril, you do not presume to alter or transpose one Word, nor rectify one false Spelling, nor so much as add or diminish one Comma or Tittle, in or to my Romance:--For if you do,--In case any of the Descendents of Curl should think fit to invade my Copy-Right, and print it over again in my Teeth, I may not be able, in a Court of Justice, to swear strictly to my own Child, after you had so large a Share in the begetting it.

In the next Place, I do not approve of your quaint Conceit at the Foot of the Title Page of my Romance,--It would only set People on finding a Page or two before I give them Leave;--and besides, all Attempts either at Wit or Humour, in that

Place, are a Forestalling of what slender Entertainment of those Kinds are prepared within: Therefore I would have it stand thus:

YORK: Printed in the Year 1759. (Price One Shilling.)

I know you will tell me, That it is set too high; and as a Proof, you will say, That this last Reply to the Dean's Answer does consist of near as many Pages as mine; and yet is all sold for Six-pence.--But mine, my dear Friend, is quite a different Story:--It is a Web wrought out of my own Brain, of twice the Fineness of this which he has spun out of his; and besides, I maintain it, it is of a more curious Pattern, and could not be afforded at the Price that his is sold at, by any honest Workman in Great-Britain.

Moreover, Sir, you do not consider, That the Writer is interested in his Story, and that it is his Business to set it a-going at any Price: And indeed, from the Information of Persons conversant in Paper and Print, I have very good Reason to believe, if he should sell every Pamphlet of them, he would inevitably be a Great Loser by it, This I believe verily, and am,

Dear Sir, Your obliged Friend and humble Servant, LAURENCE STERNE, Sutton on the Forest, Jan. 20, 1759

To Dr. TOPHAM.

Sir,

Though the Reply to the Dean of York is not declared, in the Title-Page, or elsewhere, to be wrote by you,--Yet I take that Point for granted; and therefore beg Leave, in this public Manner, to write to you in Behalf of myself; with Intent to set you right in two Points where I stand concerned in this Affair; and which I find you have misapprehended, and consequently (as I hope) misrepresented.

The First is, in respect of some Words, made use of in the Instrument, signed by Dr. Herring, Mr. Berdmore and myself.--Namely, "to the best of our Remembrance and Belief"; which Words you have caught hold of, as implying some Abatement of our Certainty as to the Facts therein attested. Whether it was so with the other two Gentlemen who signed that Attestation with me, it is not for me to say; they are able to answer for themselves, and I desire to do so for myself; and therefore I declare to you, and to all Mankind, That the Words in the first Paragraph, "to the best of our Remembrance and Belief", implied no Doubt remaining upon my Mind, nor any Distrust whatever of my Memory, from the Distance of Time;--Nor, in short, was it my Intention to attest the several Facts therein, as Matters of Belief--But as Matters of as much Certainty as a Man was capable of having, or giving Evidence to. In Consequence of this Explanation of myself, I do declare myself ready to attest the same Instrument over again, striking out the Words "to the best of our Remembrance and Belief" which I see, have raised this Exception to it.

Whether I was mistaken or no, I leave to better Judges; but I understood those Words were a very common Preamble to Attestations of Things, to which we bore the clearest Evidence;--However, Dr. Topham, as you have claimed just such another Indulgence yourself, in the Case of begging the Dean's Authority to say, what, as you affirm, you had sufficient Authority to say without, as a modest and Gentleman-like Way of Affirmation;--I wish you had spared either the one or the other of your Remarks upon these two Passages:

--Veniam petimus, demusque vicissim.

There is another Observation relating to this Instrument, which I perceive has escaped your Notice; which I take the Liberty to point out to you, namely, That the Words, "To the best of our Remembrance and Belief", if they imply any Abatement of Certainty, seem only confined to that Paragraph, and to what is immediately attested after them in it:-- For in the second Paragraph, wherein the main Points are minutely attested, and upon which the whole Dispute, and main Charge against the Dean, turns, it is introduced thus:

"We do particularly remember, That as soon as Dinner was over, &c."

In the second Place you affirm, "That it is not Paid, That Mr. Sterne could affirm he had heard you charge the Dean with a Promise, in its own Nature so very extraordinary, as of the Commissaryship of the Dean and Chapter":--To this I answer, That my true Intent in subscribing that very instrument, and I suppose of others, was to attest this very Thing; and I have just now read that Part of the Instrument over; and cannot, for my Life, affirm it either more directly or expresly, than in the Words as they there stand;--therefore please to let me transcribe them.

"But being press'd by Mr. Sterne with an undeniable Proof, That he, (Dr. Topham) did propagate the said Story, (viz: of a Promise from the Dean to Dr. Topham of the Dean and Chapter's Commissaryship)--Dr. Topham did at last acknowledge it; adding, as his Reason or Excuse for so doing, That he apprehended (or Words to that Effect) he had a Promise under the Dean's own Hand, of the Dean and Chapter's Commissaryship."

This I have attested, and what Weight the Sanction of an Oath will add to it, I am willing and ready to give.

As for Mr. Ricard's feeble Attestation, brought to shake the Credit of this firm and solemn one, I have nothing to say to it, as it is only an Attestation of Mr. Ricard's Conjectures upon the Subject.--But this I can say, That I had the Honour to be at the Deanery with the learned Counsel, when Mr. Ricard underwent that most formidable Examination you speak of,--and I solemnly affirm, That he then said, He knew nothing at all about the Matter, one Way or the other; and the Reasons he gave for his utter Ignorance, were, first, That he was then so full of Concern, at the Difference which arose between two Gentlemen, both his Friends, that he did not attend to the Subject Matter of it,--and of which he declared again he knew nothing at all. And secondly, If he had understood it then, the Distance would have put it out of his Head by this Time.

He has since scower'd his Memory, I ween; for now he says, That he apprehended the Dispute regarded something in the Dean's Gift, as he could not naturally suppose, &c. 'Tis certain, at the Deanery, he had naturally no Suppositions in his Head about this Affair; so that I with this may not prove one of the After-Thoughts you speak of, and not so much a natural as an artificial Supposition of my good Friend's.

As for the formidable Enquiry you represent him as undergoing,--let me intreat you to give me Credit in what I say upon it,--namely,--That it was as much the Reverse to every Idea that ever was couch'd under that Word, as Words can represent it to you. As for the learned Counsel and myself, who were in the Room all the Time, I do not remember that we, either of us, spoke ten Words. The Dean was the only one that ask'd Mr. Ricard what he remembered about the Affair of the Sessions Dinner; which he did in the most Gentleman-like and candid Manner,--and with an Air of as much Calmness and seeming Indifference, as if he had been questioning him about the News in the last Brussels Gazette.

What Mr. Ricard saw to terrify him so sadly, I cannot apprehend, unless the Dean's Gothic Book-Case,--which I own has an odd Appearance to a Stranger; so that if he came terrified in his Mind there, and with a Resolution not to plead, he might naturally suppose it to be a great Engine brought there on purpose to exercise the Peine fort et dure upon him.--But to be serious; if Mr. Ricard told you, That this Enquiry was most formidable, He was much to blame;--and if you have said it, without his express Information, then You are much to blame.

This is all, I think, in your Reply, which concerns me to answer:--As for the many coarse and unchristian Insinuations scatter'd throughout your Reply,--as it is my Duty to beg God to forgive you, so I do from my Heart: Believe me, Dr. Topham, they hurt yourself more than the Person they are aimed at; and when the first Transport of Rage is a little over, they will grieve you more too.

--prima est haec Ultio.

But these I hold to be no answerable Part of a Controversy;--and for the little that remains unanswered in yours,--I believe I could, in another half Hour, set it right in the Eyes of the World: But this is not my Business.--And is it is thought worth the while, which I hope it never will, I know no one more able to do it than the very Reverend and Worthy Gentleman whom you have so unhandsomely insulted upon that Score.

As for the supposed Compilers, whom you have been so wrath and so unmerciful against, I'll be answerable for it, as they are Creatures of your own Fancy, they will bear you no Malice. However, I think the more positively any Charge is made, let it be against whom it will, the better it should be supported; and therefore I should be sorry, for your own Honour, if you have not some better Grounds for all you have thrown out about them, than the mere Heat of your Imagination or Anger. To tell you truly, your Suppositions on this Head oft put me in Mind of Trim's twelve Men in Buckram, which his disordered Fancy represented as laying in Ambush in John the Clerk's House, and letting drive at him all together. I am,

SIR, Your most obedient And most humble Servant, LAWRENCE STERNE Sutton on the Forest, Jan. 20, 1759

P.S. I beg Pardon for clapping this upon the Back of the Romance,--which is done out of no Disrespect to you.--But the Vehicle stood ready at the Door,--and as I was to pay the whole Fare, and there was Room enough behind it,--it was the cheapest and readiest Conveyance I could think of.

The Codes Of Hammurabi And Moses
W. W. Davies

QTY

The discovery of the Hammurabi Code is one of the greatest achievements of archaeology, and is of paramount interest, not only to the student of the Bible, but also to all those interested in ancient history...

Religion   ISBN: *1-59462-338-4*   **Pages:132**
MSRP $12.95

The Theory of Moral Sentiments
Adam Smith

QTY

This work from 1749. contains original theories of conscience amd moral judgment and it is the foundation for systemof morals.

Philosophy ISBN: *1-59462-777-0*   **Pages:536**
MSRP $19.95

Jessica's First Prayer
Hesba Stretton

QTY

In a screened and secluded corner of one of the many railway-bridges which span the streets of London there could be seen a few years ago, from five o'clock every morning until half past eight, a tidily set-out coffee-stall, consisting of a trestle and board, upon which stood two large tin cans, with a small fire of charcoal burning under each so as to keep the coffee boiling during the early hours of the morning when the work-people were thronging into the city on their way to their daily toil...

Childrens   ISBN: *1-59462-373-2*   **Pages:84**
MSRP $9.95

My Life and Work
Henry Ford

QTY

Henry Ford revolutionized the world with his implementation of mass production for the Model T automobile. Gain valuable business insight into his life and work with his own auto-biography... "We have only started on our development of our country we have not as yet, with all our talk of wonderful progress, done more than scratch the surface. The progress has been wonderful enough but..."

Biographies/   ISBN: *1-59462-198-5*   **Pages:300**
MSRP $21.95

The Art of Cross-Examination
Francis Wellman

QTY

I presume it is the experience of every author, after his first book is published upon an important subject, to be almost overwhelmed with a wealth of ideas and illustrations which could readily have been included in his book, and which to his own mind, at least, seem to make a second edition inevitable. Such certainly was the case with me; and when the first edition had reached its sixth impression in five months, I rejoiced to learn that it seemed to my publishers that the book had met with a sufficiently favorable reception to justify a second and considerably enlarged edition. ..

Pages:412

Reference   ISBN: *1-59462-647-2*   *MSRP $19.95*

On the Duty of Civil Disobedience
Henry David Thoreau

QTY

Thoreau wrote his famous essay, On the Duty of Civil Disobedience, as a protest against an unjust but popular war and the immoral but popular institution of slave-owning. He did more than write—he declined to pay his taxes, and was hauled off to gaol in consequence. Who can say how much this refusal of his hastened the end of the war and of slavery ?

Law   ISBN: *1-59462-747-9*   **Pages:48**

MSRP $7.45

Dream Psychology Psychoanalysis for Beginners
Sigmund Freud

QTY

Sigmund Freud, born Sigismund Schlomo Freud (May 6, 1856 - September 23, 1939), was a Jewish-Austrian neurologist and psychiatrist who co-founded the psychoanalytic school of psychology. Freud is best known for his theories of the unconscious mind, especially involving the mechanism of repression; his redefinition of sexual desire as mobile and directed towards a wide variety of objects; and his therapeutic techniques, especially his understanding of transference in the therapeutic relationship and the presumed value of dreams as sources of insight into unconscious desires.

Dream Psychology
Psychoanalysis for Beginners

Sigmund Freud

Pages:196

Psychology   ISBN: *1-59462-905-6*   *MSRP $15.45*

The Miracle of Right Thought
Orison Swett Marden

QTY

Believe with all of your heart that you will do what you were made to do. When the mind has once formed the habit of holding cheerful, happy, prosperous pictures, it will not be easy to form the opposite habit. It does not matter how improbable or how far away this realization may see, or how dark the prospects may be, if we visualize them as best we can, as vividly as possible, hold tenaciously to them and vigorously struggle to attain them, they will gradually become actualized, realized in the life. But a desire, a longing without endeavor, a yearning abandoned or held indifferently will vanish without realization.

Pages:360

Self Help   ISBN: *1-59462-644-8*   *MSRP $25.45*

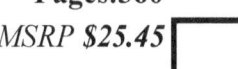

www.bookjungle.com *email: sales@bookjungle.com fax: 630-214-0564 mail: Book Jungle PO Box 2226 Champaign, IL 61825*

QTY

The Rosicrucian Cosmo-Conception Mystic Christianity *by Max Heindel*   ISBN: *1-59462-188-8*   **$38.95**
The Rosicrucian Cosmo-conception is not dogmatic, neither does it appeal to any other authority than the reason of the student. It is: not controversial, but is: sent forth in the, hope that it may help to clear...   New Age/Religion Pages 646

Abandonment To Divine Providence *by Jean-Pierre de Caussade*   ISBN: *1-59462-228-0*   **$25.95**
"The Rev. Jean Pierre de Caussade was one of the most remarkable spiritual writers of the Society of Jesus in France in the 18th Century. His death took place at Toulouse in 1751. His works have gone through many editions and have been republished...   Inspirational/Religion Pages 400

Mental Chemistry *by Charles Haanel*   ISBN: *1-59462-192-6*   **$23.95**
Mental Chemistry allows the change of material conditions by combining and appropriately utilizing the power of the mind. Much like applied chemistry creates something new and unique out of careful combinations of chemicals the mastery of mental chemistry...   New Age Pages 354

The Letters of Robert Browning and Elizabeth Barret Barrett 1845-1846 vol II   ISBN: *1-59462-193-4*   **$35.95**
by Robert Browning and Elizabeth Barrett   Biographies Pages 596

Gleanings In Genesis (volume I) *by Arthur W. Pink*   ISBN: *1-59462-130-6*   **$27.45**
Appropriately has Genesis been termed "the seed plot of the Bible" for in it we have, in germ form, almost all of the great doctrines which are afterwards fully developed in the books of Scripture which follow...   Religion/Inspirational Pages 420

The Master Key *by L. W. de Laurence*   ISBN: *1-59462-001-6*   **$30.95**
In no branch of human knowledge has there been a more lively increase of the spirit of research during the past few years than in the study of Psychology, Concentration and Mental Discipline. The requests for authentic lessons in Thought Control, Mental Discipline and...   New Age/Business Pages 422

The Lesser Key Of Solomon Goetia *by L. W. de Laurence*   ISBN: *1-59462-092-X*   **$9.95**
This translation of the first book of the "Lernegton" which is now for the first time made accessible to students of Talismanic Magic was done, after careful collation and edition, from numerous Ancient Manuscripts in Hebrew, Latin, and French...   New Age/Occult Pages 92

Rubaiyat Of Omar Khayyam *by Edward Fitzgerald*   ISBN:*1-59462-332-5*   **$13.95**
Edward Fitzgerald, whom the world has already learned, in spite of his own efforts to remain within the shadow of anonymity, to look upon as one of the rarest poets of the century, was born at Bredfield, in Suffolk, on the 31st of March, 1809. He was the third son of John Purcell...   Music Pages 172

Ancient Law *by Henry Maine*   ISBN: *1-59462-128-4*   **$29.95**
The chief object of the following pages is to indicate some of the earliest ideas of mankind, as they are reflected in Ancient Law, and to point out the relation of those ideas to modern thought.   Religion/History Pages 452

Far-Away Stories *by William J. Locke*   ISBN: *1-59462-129-2*   **$19.45**
"Good wine needs no bush, but a collection of mixed vintages does. And this book is just such a collection. Some of the stories I do not want to remain buried for ever in the museum files of dead magazine-numbers an author's not unpardonable vanity..."   Fiction Pages 272

Life of David Crockett *by David Crockett*   ISBN: *1-59462-250-7*   **$27.45**
"Colonel David Crockett was one of the most remarkable men of the times in which he lived. Born in humble life, but gifted with a strong will, an indomitable courage, and unremitting perseverance...   Biographies/New Age Pages 424

Lip-Reading *by Edward Nitchie*   ISBN: *1-59462-206-X*   **$25.95**
Edward B. Nitchie, founder of the New York School for the Hard of Hearing, now the Nitchie School of Lip-Reading, Inc, wrote "LIP-READING Principles and Practice". The development and perfecting of this meritorious work on lip-reading was an undertaking...   How-to Pages 400

A Handbook of Suggestive Therapeutics, Applied Hypnotism, Psychic Science   ISBN: *1-59462-214-0*   **$24.95**
by Henry Munro   Health/New Age/Health/Self-help Pages 376

A Doll's House: and Two Other Plays *by Henrik Ibsen*   ISBN: *1-59462-112-8*   **$19.95**
Henrik Ibsen created this classic when in revolutionary 1848 Rome. Introducing some striking concepts in playwriting for the realist genre, this play has been studied the world over.   Fiction/Classics/Plays 308

The Light of Asia *by sir Edwin Arnold*   ISBN: *1-59462-204-3*   **$13.95**
In this poetic masterpiece, Edwin Arnold describes the life and teachings of Buddha. The man who was to become known as Buddha to the world was born as Prince Gautama of India but he rejected the worldly riches and abandoned the reigns of power when...   Religion/History/Biographies Pages 170

The Complete Works of Guy de Maupassant *by Guy de Maupassant*   ISBN: *1-59462-157-8*   **$16.95**
"For days and days, nights and nights, I had dreamed of that first kiss which was to consecrate our engagement, and I knew not on what spot I should put my lips..."   Fiction/Classics Pages 240

The Art of Cross-Examination *by Francis L. Wellman*   ISBN: *1-59462-309-0*   **$26.95**
Written by a renowned trial lawyer, Wellman imparts his experience and uses case studies to explain how to use psychology to extract desired information through questioning.   How-to/Science/Reference Pages 408

Answered or Unanswered? *by Louisa Vaughan*   ISBN: *1-59462-248-5*   **$10.95**
Miracles of Faith in China   Religion Pages 112

The Edinburgh Lectures on Mental Science (1909) *by Thomas*   ISBN: *1-59462-008-3*   **$11.95**
This book contains the substance of a course of lectures recently given by the writer in the Queen Street Hail, Edinburgh. Its purpose is to indicate the Natural Principles governing the relation between Mental Action and Material Conditions...   New Age/Psychology Pages 148

Ayesha *by H. Rider Haggard*   ISBN: *1-59462-301-5*   **$24.95**
Verily and indeed it is the unexpected that happens! Probably if there was one person upon the earth from whom the Editor of this, and of a certain previous history, did not expect to hear again...   Classics Pages 380

Ayala's Angel *by Anthony Trollope*   ISBN: *1-59462-352-X*   **$29.95**
The two girls were both pretty, but Lucy who was twenty-one who supposed to be simple and comparatively unattractive, whereas Ayala was credited, as her Bombwhat romantic name might show, with poetic charm and a taste for romance. Ayala when her father died was nineteen...   Fiction Pages 484

The American Commonwealth *by James Bryce*   ISBN: *1-59462-286-8*   **$34.45**
An interpretation of American democratic political theory. It examines political mechanics and society from the perspective of Scotsman James Bryce   Politics Pages 572

Stories of the Pilgrims *by Margaret P. Pumphrey*   ISBN: *1-59462-116-0*   **$17.95**
This book explores pilgrims religious oppression in England as well as their escape to Holland and eventual crossing to America on the Mayflower, and their early days in New England...   History Pages 268

QTY

The Fasting Cure *by Sinclair Upton*   ISBN: *1-59462-222-1* **$13.95**

In the Cosmopolitan Magazine for May, 1910, and in the Contemporary Review (London) for April, 1910, I published an article dealing with my experiences in fasting. I have written a great many magazine articles, but never one which attracted so much attention... New Age/Self Help/Health Pages 164

Hebrew Astrology *by Sepharial*   ISBN: *1-59462-308-2* **$13.45**

In these days of advanced thinking it is a matter of common observation that we have left many of the old landmarks behind and that we are now pressing forward to greater heights and to a wider horizon than that which represented the mind-content of our progenitors... Astrology Pages 144

Thought Vibration or The Law of Attraction in the Thought World   ISBN: *1-59462-127-6* **$12.95**

by William Walker Atkinson   Psychology/Religion Pages 144

Optimism *by Helen Keller*   ISBN: *1-59462-108-X* **$15.95**

Helen Keller was blind, deaf, and mute since 19 months old, yet famously learned how to overcome these handicaps, communicate with the world, and spread her lectures promoting optimism. An inspiring read for everyone... Biographies/Inspirational Pages 84

Sara Crewe *by Frances Burnett*   ISBN: *1-59462-360-0* **$9.45**

In the first place, Miss Minchin lived in London. Her home was a large, dull, tall one, in a large, dull square, where all the houses were alike, and all the sparrows were alike, and where all the door-knockers made the same heavy sound... Childrens/Classic Pages 88

The Autobiography of Benjamin Franklin *by Benjamin Franklin*   ISBN: *1-59462-135-7* **$24.95**

The Autobiography of Benjamin Franklin has probably been more extensively read than any other American historical work, and no other book of its kind has had such ups and downs of fortune. Franklin lived for many years in England, where he was agent... Biographies/History Pages 332

Name	
Email	
Telephone	
Address	
City, State ZIP	

☐ **Credit Card**   ☐ **Check / Money Order**

Credit Card Number	
Expiration Date	
Signature	

Please Mail to: Book Jungle
PO Box 2226
Champaign, IL 61825
or Fax to: 630-214-0564

ORDERING INFORMATION

web*: www.bookjungle.com*
email*: sales@bookjungle.com*
fax*: 630-214-0564*
mail*: Book Jungle PO Box 2226 Champaign, IL 61825*
or PayPal *to sales@bookjungle.com*

Please contact us for bulk discounts

DIRECT-ORDER TERMS

**20% Discount if You Order
Two or More Books**
Free Domestic Shipping!
Accepted: Master Card, Visa,
Discover, American Express

www.ingramcontent.com/pod-product-compliance
Lightning Source LLC
Chambersburg PA
CBHW081202170626

46813CB00009B/3298